Airplane
yoga

Most Riverhead Books are available at special quantity discounts for bulk purchases for sales promotions, premiums, fund-raising, or educational use. Special books, or book excerpts, can also be created to fit specific needs.

For details, write: Special Markets, The Berkley Publishing Group, 375 Hudson Street, New York, New York 10014.

Airplane yoga

**Rachel Lehmann-Haupt
and Bess Abrahams**

RIVERHEAD BOOKS
NEW YORK

Every effort has been made to ensure that the information contained in this book is complete and accurate. However, neither the publisher nor the author is engaged in rendering professional advice or services to the individual reader. The ideas, procedures, and suggestions contained in this book are not intended as a substitute for consulting with your physician. All matters regarding your health require medical supervision. Neither the author nor the publisher shall be liable or responsible for any loss, injury, or damage allegedly arising from any information or suggestion in this book.

Riverhead Books
Published by The Berkley Publishing Group
A division of Penguin Group (USA) Inc.
375 Hudson Street
New York, New York 10014

Copyright © 2003 by Bess Abrahams and Rachel Lehmann-Haupt
Book design by Tiffany Kukec
Interior illustrations by Steve Karp
Cover illustrations and design by Serge Marcos

All rights reserved.
This book, or parts thereof, may not be reproduced in any form without permission. The scanning, uploading, and distribution of this book via the Internet or via any other means without permission of the publisher is illegal and punishable by law. Please purchase only authorized electronic editions, and do not participate in or encourage electronic piracy of copyrighted materials. Your support of the author's rights is appreciated.

First Riverhead trade paperback edition: September 2003

Library of Congress Cataloging-in-Publication Information
Lehmann-Haupt, Rachel.
    Airplane yoga / Rachel Lehmann-Haupt and Bess Abrahams.—
1st Riverhead trade pbk. ed.
        p. cm.
    ISBN 1-57322-352-2
    1. Yoga. 2. Air travel—Miscellanea. I. Abrahams, Bess. II. Title.

RA781.7.L455 2003
613.7'046—dc21
                                            2003047005

PRINTED IN THE UNITED STATES OF AMERICA

10 9 8 7 6 5 4 3

To Mollie Doyle, a high-flying goddess

"Each Asana and each breath is a complete journey."
—David Swenson

"Get me off this crazy thing!"
—George Jetson

Contents

Part Two: In Flight

Chapter 3: The Takeoff

Chapter 4: The Meal Tray and Movie

Chapter 5: The Bathroom Break

Part Three: The Last Leg

Chapter 6: The Landing

Chapter 7: The Baggage Area

Airplane
yoga

Introduction

re you one of those people who wish you could inspect the plane to make sure everything is in order before you take off? When you board a plane, is downing five mini-vodka bottles the first thing you want to do? Do you wish you could hide under your meal tray—or grab on to the person next to you for dear life (even if he or she is a total stranger)?

You are not alone. For most frequent fliers, twenty-first-century air travel no longer holds the romance that it did when Frank Sinatra sang "Fly Me to the Moon," "Braniff Babes" donned Emilio Pucci uniforms, and the trip was half the fun. Sure, the global economy has us flying farther and more often for business and pleasure, but today there are not a lot of options on a plane to make frequent fliers feel comfortable and relaxed. We're bombarded with airline advertisements for more legroom and wider seats, yet flights seem to get even more uncomfortable. In the past few years, "economy-class syndrome," which is a painful blood clot caused by prolonged immobility, dehydration, and cramped seating, has been a cause for alarm among many air travelers.

One of the upsides to air travel, however, is that it's a great time to escape from our busy lives. It's a time to read, watch a movie (even if it's bad), catch up on work, or just think quietly. Yet rarely do we think of it as a time to relax our bodies unless we're lucky enough to enjoy the perks of first-class massage and spa services. Most of us have to twist ourselves into the least uncomfortable positions in our tiny seats in order to get some sleep.

A few months ago, during a particularly turbulent flight from New York to Los Angeles, I found myself cramped in an economy-class seat, tired, achy, and altogether miserable. I had already spent an hour having my tweezers and underwear dusted in the security line, and then another hour sitting on the runway while the plane waited for clearance to take off. The friend with whom I was traveling suggested that I do a simple yoga stretch in my seat as a way to calm my nerves and pass the time. I laughed and immediately pictured the characters on airplane emergency cards twisted into lotus positions and the stewardess demonstrating down dogs by the emergency door and sun salutations in the aisle.

Okay, we live in an age where this five-thousand-year-old tradition has celebrities touting its benefits on the cover of magazines and football players, firefighters, and Supreme

Court justices twisting and stretching themselves into better health. But still—yoga on an airplane?

An airplane is probably the last place you think about yoga. After all, airplanes are about speed, turbulence, and moving from one place to another. Yoga is about being present in the moment, calm, and balanced. Airplanes are about cramped space and recirculated air. Yoga is about stretching and taking healthy breaths. Airplanes are about tuning out your chatty neighbor. Yoga is about tuning in and chanting "ohm."

And yet yoga is actually the perfect antidote to the stresses of travel and flight.

My pal finally convinced me to try one simple inconspicuous move. I gave in to my embarrassment and pretended to reach up toward the stewardess call button to stretch my arms. Once my arms were up there at thirty thousand feet, I took five deep breaths. It felt great. I felt the muscles in my back and arms relax and my flying jitters calm. It even helped put a little fun back into flying.

So think of *Airplane Yoga* as your emergency safety manual for in-flight stress.

This book is organized to parallel your airport experience. We take you from the long wait in the security line, and waiting area, through the duration of your flight, and all the way to the baggage claim. We recommend following the book from beginning to end as if it were a yoga class. You can also just flip through it and pick out individual moves that look good. Yoga, unlike air travel, is flexible like that. Sure you may laugh at the thought of a "Meal Tray Head Twist," "Bathroom Roll Downs," or a "Conveyor Belt Balancing Act," but these moves will actually help you arrive at your destination more relaxed—even if you choose to eat the airplane food.

Inspired by Hatha yoga techniques, Airplane Yoga exercises focus on releasing tension in your body and your mind. This book offers effective, safe—and inconspicuous—yoga moves adapted for the airplane and airport. Bess Abrahams, a certified instructor who has studied yoga in India and the United States, has considered the areas of the body that are most affected by air travel—the legs, lower back, neck, shoulders, and spine—she has also considered the amount of room that you have to do the poses. She recommends yogic breathing techniques for the plane to help nervous fliers relax, and poses to improve blood circulation. About all she hasn't figured out is a way to get by the drink cart when you really need to go to the bathroom.

Safety Tips

WARNING:

➜ Do not do standing yoga if the captain has turned on the seat-belt sign.

➜ Make sure to turn off all air-conditioning units before embarking on in-flight yoga; breathing cold air can shock the system.

➜ Don't strain yourself. Keep your belt loose.

➜ Do not do Airplane Yoga when there is turbulence.

➜ Take large items out of your pockets.

➜ Do not attempt twists if you are pregnant.

➜ Do not do yoga if you have recently had surgery.

➜ Remove your shoes whenever possible.

Part One:
takeoff

Chapter One:
The Security Line

Attention all passengers. Sure, extra security at the airport makes us feel safer, but all that sorting though suitcases for tweezers and hairpins also adds hours of time spent in lines and waiting areas. Couple that with the usual discomfort of lifting and dragging your luggage, and standing in crowded areas through each step of the security process, and you've got all the ingredients for leg, shoulder, neck, hand, and wrist tension. Here are some exercises that will help you strengthen and stretch these areas as well as occupy your mind and time—and they won't draw too much attention to you in the security line!

Note: If space permits, any postures from this section can be performed at any time during your travels (or anytime you're in a never-ending line—at the grocery store, the movies . . . you get the idea!).

wrist rolls and hand stretch

BENEFITS:
Increases circulation in your wrist joints and relieves tension in your hands.

1   Place your thumbs in your palms, make fists, and stretch your arms forward at shoulder height (or bend your elbow by your side if there is not enough room to stretch the entire arm). Do not lift your shoulders up or jut them forward.

2   **Make slow circles with your wrists in both directions, clockwise and counterclockwise, five times, making sure your palms face the floor. Complete a full slow breath with each circle you make.**

3   Open your hands, spread your fingers, and make large circles in both directions five times. Complete a full slow breath with each circle you make.

4   Make a tight fist and then pretend to throw a ball as your open your hands and spread your fingers. Repeat as many times as you'd like.

wrist flexes

BENEFITS:
Strengthens and relaxes your wrist joints after
carrying heavy luggage.

1. Stretch one arm out in front of you (or bend your elbow by your side if there is not enough room to stretch the entire arm). Flex your wrist as if you're pretending to stop runway traffic (or a 747). To increase the stretch, use the opposite hand on the palm of the outstretched hand to increase the stretch slightly (or press your palm into your travel mate's back to increase your stretch and hurry them along the line). Complete five slow deep breaths.

2. Flex your wrist in the opposite direction. To increase the stretch, use the opposite hand or your travel mate again to increase the stretch slightly. Complete five slow deep breaths.

3. Repeat with the other hand.

4. Gently shake out your wrists and hands.

CARRY-ON
shoulder shrug
and roll

BENEFITS:
Relieves shoulder tightness from the weight of
carry-on luggage.

PART ONE:

1. Inhale and lift the top of your shoulders towards your ears (keep your chin parallel to the floor).

2. Stay in this position for three breaths. Ease up if you feel a pinch in your neck.

3. Exhale and slowly draw your shoulders down as you broaden across the front of your chest and back.

PART TWO:

1. As you inhale, in one fluid movement roll your shoulders forward and up toward your ears.

2. As you exhale, roll your shoulders back and down toward the floor.

3. Repeat the full circle five times, moving in tandem with the breath, and then reverse directions.

machine massage

BENEFITS:

In case of severe security-line frustration, an arm massage can help relieve tension and increase circulation in your shoulders and arms as well as help you feel reenergized.

NOTE:

Please use this technique on your loved ones.

1 Hold a spot on your shoulder between your thumb and fingers.

2 Squeeze and release the muscles in your shoulders and begin to work your way down your arms all the way to your fingertips.

3 Repeat on the other side.

tilts

BENEFITS:
Stretches the obliques, chest, back, and neck.

1. Stand with your feet hip distance apart with your hands on your hips. Inhale and lengthen the top of your head toward the overhead lights as you push your feet into the floor.

2. Exhale and tilt forward slightly without rounding your shoulders forward. Hold your waist tight.

3. **Inhale and tilt over to the left feeling the stretch along the right side of your body. Look over the shoulder away from the direction you are tilting. Don't let your butt or ribs stick out. Complete five slow deep breaths.**

4. **Exhale and swing your fingertips behind you so they face the floor and press your lower back forward slightly as you extend your chest upward and look up. If you feel any pain in the back, ease up. Complete five slow deep breathes.**

5. Inhale and hold your waist again, tilting over to the right, feeling the stretch along the left side of your body. Look over the shoulder away from the direction

you are tilting. Don't let your butt or ribs stick out. Complete five slow deep breaths.

6   Exhale and tilt forward slightly without rounding your shoulders forward.

7   Inhale and come back to an upright position.

8   Repeat this exercise, moving in the opposite direction.

leg reviver

BENEFITS:

Walking on the balls of your feet strengthens your calves. Walking on the heels strengthens the shins. Both promote coordination and circulation. Holding still in both these positions requires focus, which calms the mind. Wiggling the fingers and toes activates the brain. Walking on the edges of your feet strengthens the muscles in the foot and is silly, promoting smiles and gaiety.

NOTE:

These exercises are an excellent antidote to cramped or stiff legs. Repeat this exercise and all other walking or standing exercises during your flight at least once!

WARNING:

These exercises should not be done if you are wearing very high heels.

PART ONE:

1   Stand with your feet slightly apart.

2   Inhale and lift your heels off the floor by pressing the balls of your feet down. Take as many mini-steps forward as the line permits and then bring your feet together and hold this position for five

deep breaths, keeping your chin parallel to the floor and the anklebones together. If the person behind you hasn't scooted up too close, try taking ministeps backward with the heels lifted.

3   Exhale and release the heels back down.

4   Try this exercise again with the toes lifted, balancing on the heels.

5   If your shoes permit, try walking and balancing on the inside and outside edge of your feet. Be careful not to strain your knees.

PART TWO:

1   Wiggle your fingers and toes.

2   Shake out the legs.

Chapter Two:
The Departure Lounge

Congratulations, you've made it through the security process. Rather than slumping in your chair and breathing shallow or partaking in the mind-numbing activity of pacing aimlessly while waiting, consider that the waiting area provides more room and time for yoga! On top of that, you now have access to a chair and a wall, which can help you do more yoga moves.

FLYING HANDS
stretch

BENEFITS:
This fun-to-do exercise strengthens your hands and fingers and improves circulation and coordination.

NOTE:
This exercise has been known to catch—and keep— the attention of children!

1 Bring your palms together into prayer position in front of your chest.

2 **While pressing your palms together, spread and fan out your fingertips away from one another until you feel a stretch at the base of your fingers. Your hands will make the shape of an *X*. Complete five slow deep breaths.**

3 **Bring your fingers back together and then pull your palms away as you keep the tips of your fingers firmly pressed together. Your hands will make a hollow "dome shape." Complete five slow deep breaths.**

4 Repeat as many times as you like, moving the hands between the *X* and "dome shape" at a faster and faster pace. See how fast you can go without letting the fingers interlace!

5 When you are finished, shake out the hands.

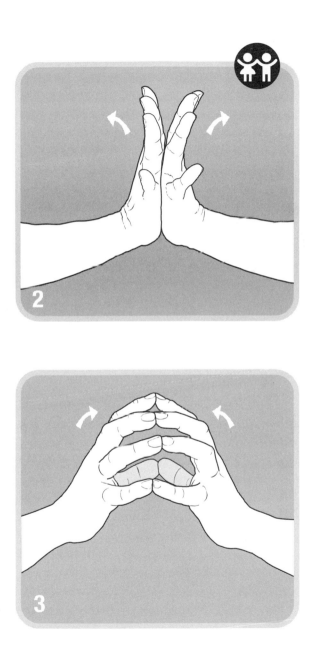

spine rolls

BENEFITS:

Increases flexibility in the spine and promotes deep breathing. Releases tension in the shoulders, head, and neck.

NOTE:

If space permits, this pose can also be done in your airplane seat.

1 Sit up straight toward the front edge of your chair with your feet flat on the floor, pointed straight ahead and hip distance apart.

2 Rest your hands facedown on your knees.

3 **Inhale and tip your hips back as you extend your chest forward and look up.**

4 **Exhale, curl your hips back, and let your shoulders and head come forward.**

5 Repeat five to ten times.

6 Find an upright position where your shoulders are over your hips and your head is stacked directly over your spine. Close your eyes and take deep breaths.

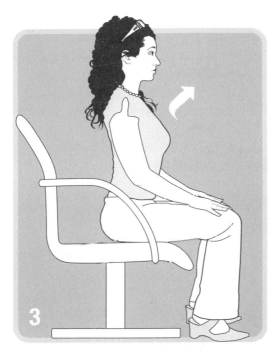

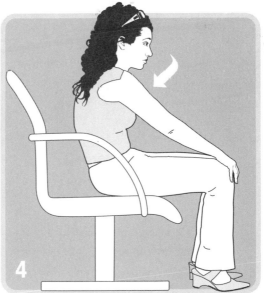

scissor kick

BENEFITS:

Invigorates tired legs and strengthens your inner
leg and abdominal muscles.

NOTE:

If space permits, this pose can also be done in your
airplane seat.

PART ONE:

1   Hold on to the sides of your seat, lean back slightly,
and sit up straight. Stretch your legs out in front of you
and lift them as high as is comfortable without slouch-
ing. Engage your abdominal muscles.

2   Inhale and separate your feet slightly.

3   **Exhale and cross the right ankle over the left as
you squeeze your inner thighs together.**

4   Inhale and uncross your legs.

5   Exhale and cross the left ankle over the right.

6   Breathing in and out, continue the movement for as
long as is comfortable.

7 Crossing one ankle over the other, hold the position for a count of ten, squeezing the legs together. Repeat with the other foot.

PART TWO:

1 With one ankle crossed over the other, try to lift the knees straight up. Don't slouch. Complete five slow deep breaths.

2 Repeat this exercise with the other ankle crossed on top.

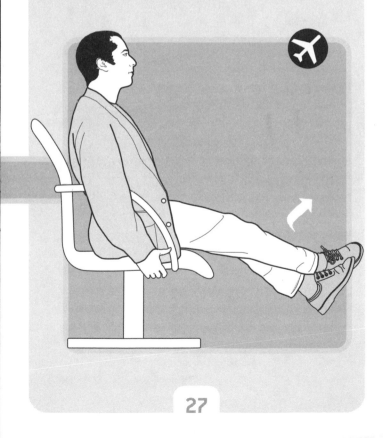

shoulder and chest openers

BENEFITS:

Stretches the chest, shoulders, neck, arms, hands, and wrists.

NOTE:

Since you are not permitted to leave your carry-on luggage unattended, stand up and place your bag on your seat or the floor in front of you to complete this exercise. If space permits, this posture can also be done in the aisle or "flight-attendant" area on the plane.

PART ONE:

1 Stand with your feet parallel and hip distance apart, with your fingers interlaced behind your back and your palms together. Make sure to distribute your weight evenly.

2 Inhale and lengthen your arms as you gently move your hands away from your lower back. Move them away only as far as you can while keeping your palms together. Keep your shoulders and hips stacked over your ankles with your tailbone lengthening toward the floor. You should feel a stretch across your chest and down the arms.

3   Exhale through your nose, lower your chin until you feel a gentle stretch in the back of your neck, and gaze softly at your carry-on luggage. Complete five full slow breaths.

PART TWO:

1   Inhale and bring your clasped hands closer to your body and your chin parallel to the floor.

2   Exhale and tilt your head to one side, feeling the stretch along the other side of your neck. To deepen the stretch, slowly move the clasped hands in the opposite direction in which you are tilting the head. Ease up if you feel strain or if you cannot complete five full slow breaths.

3   Repeat on the other side.

seated twist

BENEFITS:

This pose promotes digestion and stretches the
spine and shoulders.

NOTE:

Do not attempt this pose if you have eaten within
the last hour, are pregnant, or have had surgery
recently. If space permits, this posture can also be
done in the aisle or "flight-attendant" area on the
plane.

PART ONE:

1 Sitting forward in a seat, cross your right leg over the
left so that the knees are on top of each other and
bring your hands to your top knee.

2 Inhale and lengthen your spine as you reach the top of
your head upward.

3 **Exhale and twist your body to the right, placing
your right hand behind you or on the back of your
seat as you twist. Keep your left hand on your top
knee to stabilize the legs. Look over your right
shoulder and complete five full slow breaths.**

4 Inhale and come back to an upright position and
uncross the legs.

5   Repeat on the other side by recrossing the legs and rotating to the left.

PART TWO:

1   Sitting forward in a seat, cross your right leg over the left so that the knees are on top of each other and bring your palms together in front of your chest with the fingers pointed up.

2   Inhale and lengthen your spine as you reach the top of your head upward.

3   Exhale and rotate your chest to the right as you hook your left elbow on the outside of your top thigh. Complete five full slow breaths, continuing to rotate your chest toward the right, and look up. In order to deepen the twist, press your foot into the floor, squeeze the legs together, and press the elbow into the thigh and the thigh into the elbow.

4   Inhale and come back to an upright position and uncross the legs.

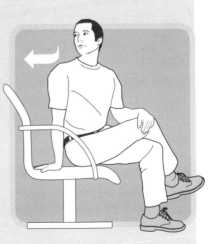

5   Switch sides by recrossing the legs and rotating to the left.

waist lengthener

BENEFITS:
Stretches your waist, shoulders, back, and arms.

NOTE:
If space permits, this posture can also been done in your airplane seat.

PART ONE:

1 Sit forward on your chair with your legs separated slightly wider than your hips in a *V* shape. Rest your palms facedown on your thighs.

2 Inhale and lengthen your back as you draw your shoulders down and broaden across your chest and shoulder blades.

3 Exhale and slide your left arm down along the inside of your left leg and place your hand on the top of your left foot or hold the ankle.

4 **Inhale and begin to open your chest toward the right, and look up as you press your feet down. Complete five full slow breaths, continuing to rotate your chest toward the right, and look up. In order to deepen the stretch at the waist, slide your right hand toward the right side of your waist and lean out to the left a little more as you**

apply slight pressure with your right hand on the waist, keeping the left hip on the chair.

5   Inhale and come back to an upright position.

6   Repeat on the other side.

PART TWO:
To make this pose more challenging, repeat the directions in Part One as described but shimmy your left shoulder underneath your left thigh and knee, and either reach your right arm up on a diagonal or take both hands behind your back, clasping them together at your lower back. Make sure to keep both hips on the chair.

wall stretch

B E N E F I T S :
Stretches the entire body and improves posture.

N O T E :
If space permits, this pose can also be done in the aisle with the hands resting against the overhead luggage compartment area.

1   Face a wall with your nose almost touching and your feet five inches away.

2   **Inhale and reach your arms above your head, placing your hands shoulder distance apart and flat. Press your hands into the wall but keep the arms straight and away from the wall.**

3   Exhale and draw your shoulders toward the floor. Make sure to look straight ahead, press your feet down, lengthen your tailbone toward the floor, and keep your rib cage from poking out to prevent crunching your lower back.

4   Complete five full slow breaths.

chair tone

BENEFITS:
Tones the thighs, butt, and legs. Strengthens the ankles and promotes concentration.

1 Lean your back against a wall. Separate your feet hip distance apart and walk them out, bending the knees so the feet come directly under your ankles. Make sure to distribute your weight evenly throughout the feet. You are making the shape of a chair.

2 Take five slow full deep breaths as you press your shoulders and back ribs against the wall. Release out of the pose if you feel discomfort in the knees or lower back.

3 Fold over your legs with your butt at the wall and the knees bent. Release the head and neck. Come up to stand slowly, using the wall for support.

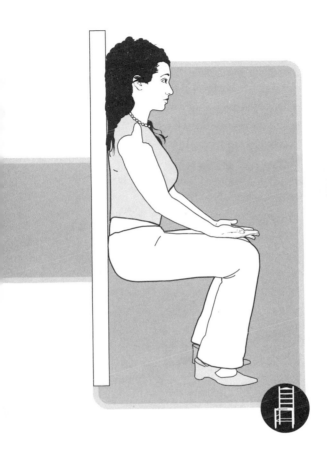

TERMINAL
lunge

BENEFITS:

Increases mobility in your hips and back, stretches and strengthens your legs, and improves balance and coordination.

NOTE:

If a wallspace is available, place the back heel at the wall for stability. If you'd like to work on improving your balance, lift your arms straight up by your ears. Even with your back heel at the wall, your entire body will have to work together to keep you balanced.

1   Come to a lunge by bending the left knee and stepping the right foot behind you with the back heel lifted. Look down at your legs and adjust the feet so that the front knee is directly over the front foot and the back leg is straight.

2   Inhale as you broaden across the chest and back, keeping the shoulders relaxed.

3   **Exhale and take hold of your waist with both hands and tip the front of your hips up slightly (if holding the waist is too difficult, rest your hands on your front thigh and soften the back knee).**

4   Complete five full slow deep breaths.

5   To come out of the pose, rest both hands on the front thigh, bend the back knee, and step forward.

6   Repeat on the second side.

warrior II

BENEFITS:
Improves breathing capacity by expanding your chest, reduces fat and stretches the muscles that surround your hips, and relieves lower backache.

PART ONE:

1   Bring your legs into a wide straddle and reach each of your arms out to either side of you at shoulder height like airplane wings. Check to see that your wrists and ankles are lined up with each other; if they are not, widen or shorten your stance as necessary.

2   Inhale and pivot on your heels so that the right foot is pointed at a ninety-degree angle away from you and the left toes are pointed in at a forty-five-degree angle. In order to protect your knees, check to make sure your back heel is behind your back toes and that the front toes are pointed straight ahead. Ground the back outer edge of your foot into the floor.

3   **Exhale and bend your right knee directly over the right foot and turn your head so you are looking over your right fingers. Keep the shoulders directly over the hips.**

4   Complete five slow full deep breaths.

To come out of the pose, inhale to straighten the bent leg, and make the feet parallel, and take an extra breath in and out before pivoting on your heels to prepare for the second side.

5

side angle

BENEFITS:
Stretches the sides of your body and promotes circulation in the feet, legs, hips, and shoulders.

1. Bring your legs into a wide straddle and reach both your arms out to either side of you at shoulder height like airplane wings. Check to see that your wrists and ankles are lined up with each other; if they are not, widen or shorten your stance as necessary.

2. Inhale and pivot on your heels so that the right foot is at a ninety-degree angle pointed away from you and the left toes are pointed in at a forty-five-degree angle. In order to protect your knees, check to make sure your back heel is behind your back toes and that the front toes are pointed straight ahead. Ground the back outer edge of your foot into the floor.

3. Exhale and bend your right knee directly over the right foot and lean out over the thigh, resting your right forearm on your right thigh. Don't let the knee track inward.

4. **Inhale and reach your left arm by your left ear (if taking the arm alongside the ear is too strenuous, take the left hand to your left waist). You should feel a stretch along the entire left side of your body as well as throughout both legs and the hips.**

5   Complete five slow full deep breaths.

6   To come out of the pose, inhale to straighten the bent leg and make the feet parallel, and take an extra breath in and out before pivoting on your heels to prepare for the second side.

Part Two:
in flight

Chapter Three:
The Takeoff

Welcome aboard. Just because you're in the air doesn't mean your yoga class has to stop. For many travelers, this is the most stressful part of the journey, so yoga in-flight is even more beneficial than it was in the terminal. While you are seated in your airplane seat, there are many things you can do to relieve tension, increase circulation, and pass the time, and then there is the aisle, overhead luggage compartment, bathroom, and "flight-attendant" area that can be of use. If your neighbors never seem to leave their seats, have them join you! It'll be a challenge, considering you don't have that much room, but these moves will get you through that two-hour delay on the runway, not to mention turbulence, bad air, uncomfortable movie viewing—and the food.

counting meditation

BENEFITS:

Calms your mind by promoting concentration and breathing.

NOTE:

Try this meditation technique to calm your nerves and pass the time before takeoff. This technique is also recommended for turbulence.

1   Close your eyes.

2   As you breathe in, focus on the sensation on the outer edges of your nostrils. As you breathe out, focus on the sensation on the inside edges of your nostrils.

spine rolls

BENEFITS:

If there has been a delay and you feel like bolting off the plane, you can repeat the spine rolls from Chapter 2. Imagine you are rolling off to a smooth flight. Spine rolls are an excellent exercise to do at any time during the flight.

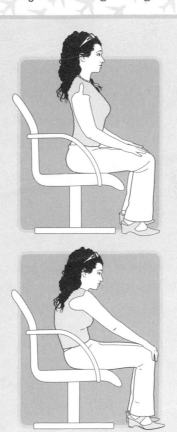

head tilts

BENEFITS:

Stretches and relieves tension in your neck and jaw.

1 Inhale and sit up straight in your seat with your feet flat on the floor.

2 **Exhale and tilt your head to one side. Complete five slow full deep breaths. To work different parts of the neck, make small circles with your chin in both directions with the head tilted. To relieve tension in the jaw, move the lower jaw from side to side and forward and back.**

3 Inhale to bring the head back to center.

4 Repeat on the other side.

5 Exhale and gently tilt your head forward, using your hands at the back of your head to increase the stretch. Don't overdo it! Complete five slow full deep breaths.

6 Inhale and tilt your head upward into a comfortable stretch for the front of your neck. Use your hands at the base of your skull to support the head. Complete five slow full deep breaths and then use your fingertips to give yourself a massage at the base of your skull.

7 Release your head back to the upright position.

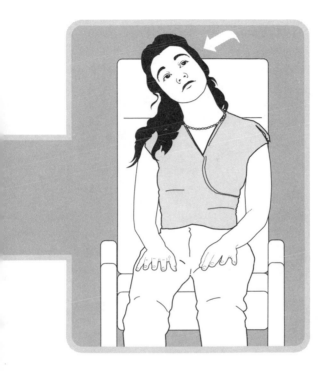

AIRPLANE
arm stretch

BENEFITS:
Stretches the shoulders, arms, and spine and lengthens the waist.

NOTE:
This pose can also be done standing.

1 Interlace your fingers in front of your chest. Invert your palms to face away from you and stretch the arms out at shoulder height.

2 **Inhale and lift your arms overhead.**

3 Complete five slow full deep breaths. Make sure to keep your chin parallel to the floor, your palms parallel to the ceiling, and the shoulders drawing down while you expand and broaden across the chest and shoulder blades. Don't strain.

4 Upon exhaling slowly release the arms to your sides.

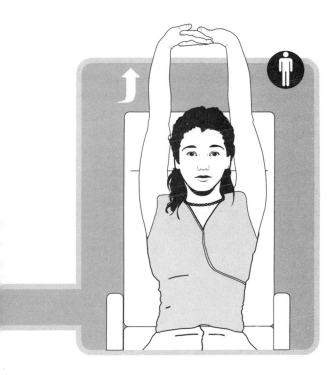

chest opener

BENEFITS:
Stretches your chest and shoulders and
strengthens your arm muscles.

1   Sit forward in your seat.

2   **Puff your chest out and pull your elbows straight back so that they touch the back of your seat. Contract your arm muscles but keep the face relaxed.**

3   Look over the top of the seat in front of you and complete five slow deep full breaths.

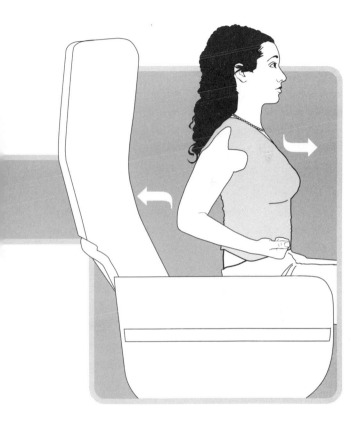

OVERHEAD LUGGAGE COMPARTMENT
twist

BENEFITS:
Stretches the shoulders, arms, and spine and promotes digestion.

NOTE:
This pose can also be done standing.

1 Interlace your fingers in front of your chest. Invert your palms to face away from you and stretch the arms out at shoulder height.

2 Inhale and lift your arms overhead. Make sure to keep your chin parallel to the floor, your palms parallel to the ceiling, and the shoulders drawing down while you expand and broaden across the chest and shoulder blades. Don't strain.

3 **Exhale and twist your upper body to the right. Complete five full deep slow breaths.**

4 Inhale and bring your chest back to the center.

5 Exhale and twist to the left. Complete five full deep slow breaths.

6 Inhale back to center and slowly release the arms.

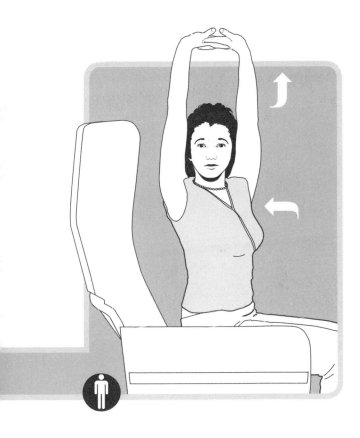

wrist release

BENEFITS:
Releases tension in the wrists.

1   Hold the barf bag with your hands slightly separated.

2   **Breathing in and out, pretend you are ringing out a towel, rotating the wrists in opposite directions.**

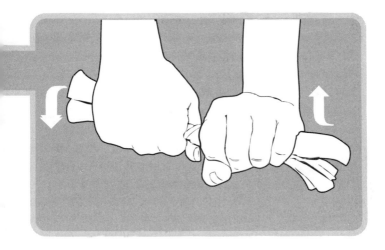

belly toner

BENEFITS:
Develops abdominal strength.

1   Sit up straight in your chair with your feet flat on the
    floor.

2   **Inhale and lift both feet a few inches off the floor
    without slouching and draw the inside edges of
    your legs and feet together. Complete five slow
    full deep breaths.**

3   Exhale to release the feet back to the floor.

thigh tone

BENEFITS:
Develops sexy stewardess legs and releases
tension in the ankles.

1   Sit up straight in your chair with your feet flat on the
    floor.

2   **Inhale and lift one of your thighs a few inches
    away from the seat as you press the foot of the
    opposite leg into the floor. Imagine that your thigh
    is being drawn toward the overhead lights by a
    puppet string. Complete five slow full deep
    breaths.**

3   Breathing in and out, circle your ankle in both direc-
    tions three to five times.

4   Exhale to release the foot back to the floor.

5   Repeat the exercise with your other leg.

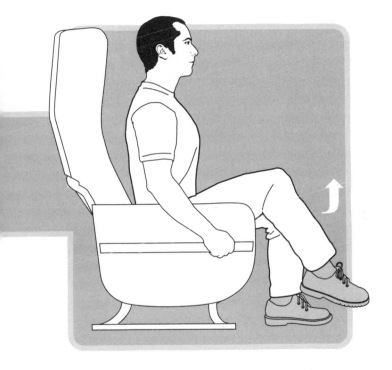

RED-EYE
foot flex

BENEFITS:

It's 3 A.M. and you're somewhere over Iowa. You try to curl up in your seat, but you just can't seem to find a comfortable position. Try a simple foot flex in order to stretch the lower leg, soles of your feet, and your toes. This will increase your circulation and relax your ankle joints.

NOTE:
Take off your shoes.

1 Sit up straight in your chair with your feet flat on the floor.

2 Inhale and slowly begin to peel your feet off the floor starting with the toes until just your heels are resting on the floor. Spread and wiggle your toes. Complete five slow full deep breaths.

3 Exhale and slowly lower the feet back down.

Chapter Four:
The Meal Tray and Movie

Airline food may be justly disparaged, but the meal tray as a "yoga prop" is definitely underrated. Before your meal or the movie, why not try a relaxing stretch or meditation as a way to calm your mind and promote digestion? One of the many benefits of meditation is that it makes you focus on the moment. When we are more mindful we are less likely to overeat or consider radical changes in our personality or appearance in order to emulate the characters in the in-flight movie.

head twist and neck tilt

BENEFITS:
Relieves tension in the jaw, neck, and shoulders.

1   Release your meal tray from its upright and locked position.

2   Put your chin in your left hand and lean your elbow on your meal tray.

3   **Lean your head into your hand so your head tilts to the left. Close your eyes and complete five slow full deep breaths. The key to maximizing this stretch is to create space between your shoulders and your ears by drawing the shoulders down as you broaden across the chest and shoulder blades.**

4   With your eyes closed, gently open and close your mouth to relieve tension in your jaw. If your annoying neighbor gets up to go to the bathroom, make a "haa" sound as you open your mouth and exhale. Move the bottom jaw side to side and back and forth.

5   Repeat on second side.

shoulder release

BENEFITS:
Relaxes your shoulders.

1 Release your meal tray from its upright and locked position.

2 Sit up straight in your chair with your feet flat on the floor.

3 **Exhale and gently press your palms underneath the meal tray as you drop your shoulders down. Since the meal tray provides no resistance, try to use as light a touch as possible.**

meditation

BENEFITS:
Calms the nervous system and promotes digestion
and deep breathing.

NOTE:
If you have a tendency to overeat or eat airplane
food even when it doesn't taste good, try this
meditation exercise before your food arrives and
again after you've eaten, noticing how you feel
before and after the meal.

1 Close your eyes softly.

2 Count your breaths backward from ten to zero.

When you get to zero, start counting backward from
3 ten again. If you lose your place, simply start back at
ten.

MOVIE
eye soother

BENEFITS:
Strengthens the eye muscles and soothes
the eyes.

NOTE:
As a result of viewing obstructions and poor light-
ing caused by insufficiently shade-conscientious
passengers, you may experience eyestrain,
headaches, or shoulder and neck tension during
or after the movie. In addition to doing these eye
exercises, drinking water during the movie and
repeating any of the head, neck, or
shoulder stretches is recommended.

NOTE:
For all of these exercises move slowly and
keep the head still.

PART ONE:

1   Draw a straight line with your eyes from floor to ceiling
and back down again. Repeat three times then close
the eyes.

2   Draw a straight line with your eyes from side to
side. Repeat three times then close the eyes.

3 Trace the numbers of a clock in both the clockwise and counterclockwise directions. When you are finished, close the eyes.

4 Trace a sideways figure eight sign with your eyes. When you are finished, close the eyes.

PART TWO:

1 Rub your palms together quickly, creating heat between your hands.

2 Keep your fingers together and cup the hands over your eyes. The heat and darkness will help the eyes relax.

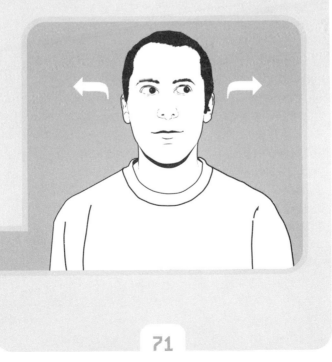

Chapter Five:
The Bathroom Break

The following moves will help you relax instead of worrying about getting there—even when your snoring neighbor is driving you crazy and you've read all the magazines.

Warning: Fliers should get up from their seats every two hours to prevent "economy-class syndrome."

lean

BENEFITS:
Stretches the sides of your torso and increases
circulation in the arms.

1   Stand with your feet underneath your hips and pointed
straight ahead.

2   Inhale and fully extend your arms overhead with your
palms facing each other.

3   **Exhale and lean out to your left. You can either
lower the left arm by your side or use the left hand
to hold on to the right wrist (the right palm should
face up). You should feel the stretch along the
entire right side of your body. Complete five slow
full deep breaths. Do not allow your back to over-
arch.**

4   Inhale and come back to center.

5   Exhale as you lean out to the right, repeating the exercise on the other side.

BATHROOM
roll downs

1   Stand with your feet underneath your hips and pointed straight ahead.

2   **As you exhale, curl forward, leading with the top of your head. Make sure your head and neck roll down with the rest of you. Keep the knees slightly bent.**

3   Gently shake out your arms, head, neck, and shoulders. Hang over your legs as long as comfortable with bent knees.

4   As you inhale, begin to roll back up. Make sure to keep your knees slightly bent. The head comes up last.

5   Stand tall with the eyes closed, feeling the vertebrae stacked one on top of the other. Complete five slow full deep breaths.

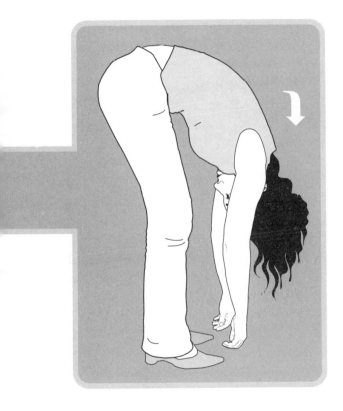

butt toner

BENEFITS:
Tones your butt, legs, and belly and strengthens your ankles.

PART ONE:

1 Stand with your feet underneath your hips and pointed straight ahead.

2 **Bend your knees and reach your arms up overhead with the palms separated. Imagine you are sitting in a chair (if this is too strenuous for you, rest your hands on your thighs). Lengthen your tailbone toward your heels, activate the thigh muscles, and keep drawing the shoulders down as you broaden across the chest and shoulder blades.**

3 Complete five slow full deep breaths in this position.

4 Exhale, come back up to stand, and release your arms by your sides.

PART TWO:

1 Hang over your legs with the knees bent. Become like a rag doll.

2 Gently shake out the head, neck, shoulders, and legs.

3 Slowly roll up to stand. Imagine stacking your vertebrae one on top of the other.

dipping lunges

BENEFITS:
Invigorates the legs and increases circulation throughout the body.

1 **Take a step forward, keeping the back heel lifted and the front knee bent.**

2 Step into minilunges with each stride you take down the aisle. Swing your arms back and forth as you do this.

eagle pose

BENEFITS:
Promotes balance, stretches legs, hips, shoulders, arms, and hands.

1. Stand up straight, with your feet underneath your hips and pointed straight ahead.

2. Step your right foot over the left, bringing both feet flat on the floor (if this is not possible or comfortable, just bring the toes to touch the floor). Squeeze the inner thighs together. Balance.

3. Wrap your arms by placing the left elbow on top of the right, then rotate the palms to face each other with the fingertips pointed up, and bring the hands to touch.

4. **Inhale and lift the elbows away from your chest and the fingers toward the fluorescent lights. You should feel the stretch across your shoulder blades. Do not strain. Keep inner legs firm and the tops of the shoulders away from your ears. Complete five slow full deep breaths.**

5. Repeat on other side.

counting meditation

BENEFITS:
Increases circulation in your legs and
calms the mind.

1 Walk slowly down the aisle, focusing on rolling through
   your foot as you step.

2 Count your steps.

3 For an extra challenge, try to slow down your steps so
   much that they match your inhalations and exhala-
   tions.

Part Three:
the last leg

Chapter Six:
The Landing

Bored, frustrated, or otherwise put out? Take a deep breath, fasten your seat belt, and do the following moves to calm your jitters and increase circulation throughout your body.

reviver

BENEFITS:
Releases tension throughout the body and
increases circulation.

1   Roll back and forth on your feet.

2   Tap your toes side to side.

3   Squeeze and then release different parts of your body
    without using your hands, working from your toes up.
    For example, squeeze and release your toes, then your
    foot, calves, thighs, buttocks, etc.

4   **Breathe in through your mouth and puff out your
    cheeks as you close your lips. Swish the air
    around your mouth as if you were using mouth-
    wash. To release, open the mouth and make the
    sound *ahhhh*. Stick out your tongue if you dare!**

5   Move your tongue around the inside of your mouth.

light breathing

BENEFITS:

You're about to land, and anxiety has you biting your nails and clenching your teeth. When the little bell rings telling you that the captain has turned on the seat-belt sign, think of it as a bell that is meant to bring your mind into focus. This breathing exercise will relax your mind and strengthen your lungs. It's great for in-flight turbulence, too.

1   Close your eyes.

2   Through the nose, take three small sips of breath into your body, focusing on expanding your lower belly, then the midchest, and finally the upper chest.

3   Through the nose, begin exhaling as you focus on releasing the breath from the upper chest, midchest, and lower belly. Remember to keep your face and shoulders relaxed.

4   Try to increase the duration of the exhale. Ideally, you would like the inhale to take three seconds and the exhale to take five seconds.

5   Repeat ten times or until you feel your tension subsiding with each exhalation.

FACE
lift

BENEFITS:
Relieves tension and improves circulation
to the face.

1 **Using small circular movements with your fingertips, massage your face, starting at the bottom of your face and working upward. Don't forget the ears and skull.**

2 Close your eyes and visualize your face completely expressionless.

3 Tighten your face up so you look like a raisin and then open your mouth wide, stick out your tongue, and pretend you're a lion.

Chapter Seven:
The Baggage Area

Welcome to wherever you are. Please don't unfasten your seat belt and stand until the plane has stopped taxiing. Why not think about taking advantage of the walk off the plane to the luggage retrieval area and the curbside where you will inevitably wait for transportation?

pep walks

BENEFITS:
These exercises will entertain you as well as strengthen your legs.

Walk off the plane backward. When you get to the exit, turn around and walk off.

Or

Walk off the plane on your tiptoes.

Or

Walk off the plane by tapping the inside edge of one foot against the other with each step.

Or

Repeat the Aisle Counting Meditation from Chapter 5, noticing everything as you pass, being grateful that it's the last time you'll be seeing it.

balancing act

BENEFITS:
Promotes balance and concentration, and
stretches the thighs and groin.

1 Stand with your feet together, arms relaxed at your sides.

2 **Inhale and bend your right foot behind you, bringing the heel toward your right buttock with the right hand. Keep your knees together.**

3 Exhale and press your left foot down as you press the right foot into your hand until you feel a stretch across the front of your right thigh.

4 Breathing in and out, gaze forward and complete five slow full deep breaths. Don't arch your back or stick your ribs out.

5 Repeat with the left foot.

leg stretch

BENEFITS:
Stretches the Achilles tendon and the calves,
and strengthens the shins.

1 In a nontraffic area, find a curbside or step where you can comfortably place your toes on a level higher than the heels.

2 Inhale and lift one heel off the ground.

3 **Exhale and slowly return the heel to the ground, feeling the stretch along the calf as you lift the opposite heel up.**

4 Continue this movement of "walking," alternating the feet.

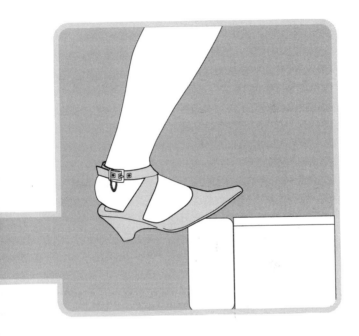

LUGGAGE
arms

BENEFITS:
Stretches your arms, chest, and back for that long
luggage haul to your final destination.

NOTE:
You'll need room to stretch your arms out
to the sides.

1 Stand up straight, with your feet under your hips and pointed straight ahead.

2 Inhale and open your arms out to the side at shoulder height with the palms facing forward. You will look as if you are about to receive someone in a big hug, and you should feel the stretch along the front of your body and down the arms.

3 Exhale and give yourself a hug by crossing one arm over the other.

4 Repeat this exercise by uncrossing and crossing the arms. Make sure to alternate which arm goes on top when you give yourself a hug.

Conclusion

Thank you for flying with *Airplane Yoga*. As you know, air travel warps our sense of time and place, and it causes mental and physical sluggishness. By following these yoga exercises, you have helped yourself to alleviate stress and to focus on the present moment. We hope that you have enjoyed your flight and that Airplane Yoga has put a little fun back into your flying experience. We will conclude your flight with a brief discussion of the general benefits of yoga, yoga tips for travel, and information regarding how to find out more about yoga, or even where to find a yoga class when you are on the ground. Thank you for coming to us for all your Airplane Yoga needs.

Benefits of Yoga

B e prepared for the following benefits: improved physical well-being, easier adjustment to sleep disruption caused by jet lag, better digestion, and less stress. Yoga exercises, if done regularly, will cultivate strength and promote flexibility. Improved muscle tone will make sitting through long trips easier.

Deep breathing helps alleviate the fatigue or sleeping difficulties that result from jet lag. It will also improve your digestion and help you relax. Our bodies react to cramped space and stagnant air by contracting. Mind activity tends to follow the breathing rate. The body loosens up and settles down as it gets more oxygen. By moving and breathing slowly and deeply, you are creating a feeling of space in your body and mind. Yoga exercises also help to increase awareness. Focusing your concentration will help you release tension.

Tips for Frequent
Airplane Yoga Fliers

1. Try doing your favorite exercises even on days when you do not travel.

2. Rest if you need to.

3. Be sure to travel in comfortable clothing (especially shoes).

4. Try to get onto the sleeping and eating pattern of your destination before you leave.

5. Don't overeat on your flight. Overeating causes sluggishness in the body and mind because your system is overworked digesting food.

6. Drink plenty of water. Staying hydrated in-flight will prevent stress and dehydration.

7. Bring your own hydrating snacks, such as celery and oranges.

8. Listening to music can intensify your Airplane Yoga experience. Here are some recommended CDs to get into the Airplane Yoga groove.

Wah!, *Hidden in the Name*

Diana Rogers, *Unveiled*

Henryk Górecki, Symphony no. 3

Ravi Shankar, *Chants of India*

El-Hadra, *The Mystic Dance*

Krishna Das, *Breath of the Heart*

Gabrielle Roth and The Mirrors, *Refuge*

Master Charles, *Om: The Reverberation of Source*

Jai Uttal, *Footprints*

Brian Eno, *Ambient Music for Airports*

Internet Resources

Here are some Internet resources to accommodate the traveling yogi:

www.self-realization.com/yoga directory: a guide to yoga centers, associations, teachers, studios, and ashrams around the world.

www.americanyogaassociation.com: advice on how to select a yoga teacher.

www.yogasite.com: information on different yoga styles, directory of teachers, product information, listing of events and workshops, information on yoga for specific health concerns.

www.yrec.com: the site for the Yoga Research and Education Center.

www.yogajournal.com: official *Yoga Journal* magazine website.

www.yimag.com: articles and resource directory from *Yoga International* magazine.

About the Authors

Rachel Lehmann-Haupt writes about cultural trends. Her work has appeared in *The New York Times, The New York Observer,* and numerous other publications.

Bess Abrahams holds teaching certifications from the Jivamukti Yoga School, Next Generation Yoga Center for Kids and the Yoga For Special Needs Children program at the Integral Yoga Institute. She is a continual student of anatomy and a devoted student of the Ashtanga vinyasa system as taught by Sri K. Patabbhi Jois. She has studied in India and America under the guidance of many master and senior yoga teachers in the traditions of Ashtanga vinyasa, Jivamukti method, Iyengar Yoga and Sanskrit.